Grizzwold

Story and pictures by
Syd Hoff

An I CAN READ Book

Library of Congress Catalog Card Number: 63-14366
ISBN 0-06-022480-0
ISBN 0-06-022481-9 (lib. bdg.)
ISBN 0-06-444057-5 (pbk.)
First Harper Trophy edition, 1984.

16 17 PC/WOR 10 9 8

Grizzwold

In the far North
lived a bear named Grizzwold.

Grizzwold was so big

three rabbits could sit in his footprint.

When he went fishing,

the river only came to his knees.

Other bears had no trouble
going into caves to sleep.
Grizzwold always got stuck.

8

He had to sleep out in the open.

But he didn't mind.

He had a nice coat of fur

to keep him warm.

9

No other animal dared wake him.

One morning there was a loud noise
in the forest.
All the other bears ran away.

Grizzwold went to see what it was.

He saw men chopping down trees.

"Timber!" they shouted.

13

"What's the big idea?" asked Grizzwold.

"What are you doing to my forest?"

14

"We are sorry," said the men.

"We have to send these logs

down the river to the mill.

They will be made into paper."

"I can't live in a forest
with no trees," said Grizzwold.

16

He went to look

for a new place to live.

"Do you know

where there is a nice forest?"

he asked.

"You won't find one up here,"
said a mountain goat.

"Do you know

where there is a nice forest?"

he asked.

"You won't find one here,"

said a prairie wolf.

21

"Do you know

where there is a nice forest?"

he asked.

"Boy, are you lost!"

said a desert lizard.

23

Grizzwold looked until he saw houses.

"What can I do here?" he asked.

"You can be a bearskin rug,"
said some people.

They let him into their house.

Grizzwold lay down on the floor.

The people stepped all over him.

"Ow! I don't like this," said Grizzwold.

He left the house.

Grizzwold saw a light pole.

"I'll climb that tree," he said.

31

"I was here first," said a cat.

He chased Grizzwold away.

Grizzwold saw a dog.

"Can't you read?" asked the dog.

34

He chased Grizzwold away.

Grizzwold saw people going to a dance.

The people wore masks.

Grizzwold went to the dance too.

"You look just like a real bear,"
said the people.

"Thank you," said Grizzwold.

38

The people started to dance.

Grizzwold started to dance too.

"It is time to take off our masks,"
said somebody.

All the people took off their masks.

"Take off yours too,"

they said to Grizzwold.

"I can't," he said.

"This is my real face."

"You don't belong here,"

said the people.

"You belong in the zoo."

Grizzwold went to the zoo.

The bears were begging for peanuts.

Grizzwold begged too.

"Please don't stay," said the bears.

"We need all the peanuts we get.

Try the circus."

Grizzwold went to the circus.

They put skates on him.

He went FLOP!

They put him on a bicycle.

He went CRASH!

51

They tried to make him
stand on his head.

He couldn't do that either!

"I guess it takes practice,"

said Grizzwold.

"It sure does," said the trained bears.

54

Grizzwold tried to rest.

"You can't park here,"

said a policeman.

"I'll find a place to park,"

said Grizzwold.

He ran until he came to a nice forest.

"I'm very glad to be here," he said.

"We are very glad you are here too,"
said some hunters.

They took aim.

"Don't shoot!" said a ranger.

"This is a national park.

No hunting allowed."

The hunters left.

"Thank you," said Grizzwold.

"You will be safe here,"

said the ranger.

"People cannot shoot animals here.

They can only shoot pictures."

All the people

wanted to take Grizzwold's picture.

He was the biggest bear

they had ever seen.

"Thanks for posing for us,"

they said.

"This is the life for me,"

said Grizzwold.

He was very happy.